MY SOUL HAS BEEN ABUSED

BY: JANET K HOWARD

Table of Contents

INTRODUCTION

TO ALL WHO READ MY BOOKS, I AM INSPIRED BY GOD TO SHARE THE WISDOM AND KNOWLEDGE THAT GOD HIMSELF HAS POURED INTO ME. I WANT TO SHARE MY PERSONAL EXPERIENCES IN LIFE AND HOW I DEALT WITH BEING HURT AND WOUNDED SO DEEPLY THAT ONLY GOD COULD HEAL THESE WOUNDS AND SCARS OF MY ABUSED SOUL.

PEOPLE WALK AROUND WITH A HOLE IN THEIR SOUL, NOT REALLY KNOWING THAT THEY ARE WOUNDED AND SCARRED SO DEEP DOWN INSIDE THEM, AND NOT KNOWING HOW TO DEAL WITH THEIR EMOTIONS, BEHAVIOR, AND FEELINGS THAT CAUSE A PERSON TO STAY BROKEN.

I HOPE THAT THIS BOOK WILL HELP AND ENCOURAGE OTHERS TO TRY AND LOOK AT AND DEAL WITH WHAT IS INSIDE THEIR HEARTS SO THAT THEY WILL BE ABLE TO BE HEALED.

ONCE YOU REALIZE THAT YOUR SOUL HAS A HOLE IN IT AND YOU'VE ALLOWED THESE FEELINGS TO GO UNNOTICED, YOU MUST SEEK GOD TO FORGIVE YOU AND REPENT OF ALL SINS. ALLOW GOD TO RESTORE YOU PHYSICALLY, MENTALLY,

EMOTIONALLY, AND SPIRITUALLY. SOME PEOPLE NEED SEXUAL HEALING FROM BEING RAPED, MOLESTED, OR PHYSICALLY BEATEN DOWN BY THE THINGS THAT HAVE HAPPENED IN THEIR LIVES. IT STARTS WITH FORGIVENESS AND DEALING WITH WHAT ONCE HURT YOU. SO PLEASE DON'T SHUT PEOPLE OUT OF YOUR LIFE WHO GOD HAS PLACED THERE TO HELP YOU HEAL. I THOUGHT I DIDN'T NEED ANYONE, BUT THAT'S NOT TRUE. WE ALL NEED SOMEBODY TO BE THERE, TO HELP AND SUPPORT US WHILE WE ARE HEALING. I THANK GOD FOR ALL THE PEOPLE HE HAS PLACED IN MY LIFE, BUT YOU MUST ALSO BE CAREFUL BECAUSE THE DEVIL WILL SEND PEOPLE INTO A PERSON'S LIFE TO DISTRACT THEM FROM THEIR PURPOSE AND PREVENT THEM FROM HEALING.

SATAN COMES TO KILL, STEAL, AND DESTROY PEOPLE'S LIVES, BUT GOD COMES SO THAT WE MIGHT HAVE LIFE AND HAVE IT MORE ABUNDANTLY. (JOHN 10:10)

TRUST GOD FOR YOUR HEALING SO YOU CAN LOVE AND LIVE WITHOUT PAIN AND BE FREE OF THE DEVIL'S STRONGHOLDS

ACKNOWLEDGMENT

GIVING ALL THE GLORY TO GOD FOR MY LIFE AND FOR GIVING ME THE ABILITY TO WRITE AND BECOME AN AUTHOR. THANK YOU, LORD GOD, FOR WHAT YOU HAVE DONE IN MY LIFE AND FOR WHAT YOU ARE GOING TO DO IN MY LIFE. THANK YOU FOR ALL THE MANY BLESSINGS YOU HAVE PROMISED ME.

I KNOW THAT WHAT GOD HAS FOR ME IS FOR ME. I WILL NOT WORRY ABOUT WHAT'S COMING, BUT I WILL KEEP BELIEVING IN GOD TO MEET MY EVERY NEED AND GIVE ME THE DESIRES OF MY HEART. AMEN.

I WANT TO THANK THE COFFEE CLUB, SIDNEY (MY SON), JASPER (MY NEPHEW), STEVEN (MY SON), FAITH (MY NIECE), AND LAST BUT NOT LEAST, MY COUSIN JAY, FOR CREATING THE COFFEE CLUB WHERE NO SUBJECT IS OFF-LIMITS, FOR ALL THE SUPPORT, BOTH FINANCIAL AND OTHERWISE, AND FOR ALL THE LAUGHTER AND LOVE I RECEIVE FROM YOU GUYS ON A DAILY BASIS.

TO MY SISTER, VALARIE TAYLOR, FOR YOUR PRAYERS AND ENCOURAGING WORDS, FOR ALWAYS COMING THROUGH

WHEN I REALLY NEEDED YOU, AND TO MY BROTHER-IN-LAW, BEAU TAYLOR, FOR BEING SO UNDERSTANDING WHEN I NEEDED MY SISTER. MUCH LOVE, BEAU, LOVE YOU, BRO.

TO MY MOTHER, MAE CRAWFORD, I LOVE YOU TO THE MOON AND BACK. MAY GOD CONTINUE TO BLESS YOU WITH A LONG AND FULFILLING LIFE.

TO MY AUNTIE SHIRLEY DOUGLAS, FOR LISTENING TO ME IN THE MIDNIGHT HOURS WHEN EVERYONE ELSE IS ASLEEP, AND TO MY FAMILY MEMBERS AND FRIENDS I DIDN'T NAME, I LOVE YOU ALL. MAY GOD BLESS YOU.

TO MY LOVE AGENT, I DEDICATE THIS BOOK TO YOU. THE DEDICATION IS IN THE BACK OF THIS BOOK. THANK YOU FOR BEING A PART OF MY LIFE WHEN I REALLY NEEDED A SPECIAL FRIEND. MAY GOD BLESS YOU AND GRANT YOU THE DESIRES OF YOUR HEART, AND MAY ALL YOUR DREAMS COME TRUE. MUCH LOVE AND ALL THE HAPPINESS IN THE WORLD.

ALONE IN THE GARDEN

ADAM, YOU WANTED TO BE LEFT ALONE IN THE GARDEN OF EDEN. YOU SAID TO LEAVE YOU ALONE IN THE GARDEN OF EDEN, ALONE. I HURT YOU SO BADLY THAT YOU WANTED ME TO GO AWAY. I DIDN'T MEAN TO HURT YOU. I WANTED TO BE WITH YOU; YOU WERE MY SOULMATE, AND I LOVED YOU WITH ALL MY HEART AND SOUL. I LOVED YOU WITH EVERYTHING I HAD INSIDE OF ME UNTIL YOU LEFT ME ALONE IN THE GARDEN OF EDEN FOR SOMEONE WHO DIDN'T EVEN LOVE ME, BUT WHO SHOWED ME FALSE LOVE AND CAUSED ME TO SIN.

YOU LEFT ME ALONE, AND I WAS HURT. I SEARCHED FOR LOVE BUT COULD NEVER FIND THE LOVE THAT I SO DESIRED. THE LOVE I HAD FOR YOU I COULD NEVER FIND IN ANYONE ELSE, NO MATTER HOW HARD I TRIED. NOW YOU WANT ME TO LEAVE YOU ALONE IN THE GARDEN OF EDEN? LIKE YOU LEFT ME WOUNDED, HURT, AND ABUSED, I CAME TO YOU TO TRY AND MEND YOUR BROKEN HEART ONLY TO FIND THAT IT WAS MY HEART THAT NEEDED MENDING. IT WAS YOU WHO BROKE MY HEART. WE KEPT GOING BACK AND FORTH ABOUT WHO DID WHAT, WHY AND WHEN. SO NOW YOU WANT ME TO LEAVE

YOU ALONE IN EDEN SO YOU CAN HEAL? I'M SORRY FOR ALL THE PAIN I CAUSED. I'M SORRY FOR HURTING YOU. I HURT YOU, AND YOU HURT ME TOO, SO I GUESS THIS IS WHERE I LET YOU GO AND SAY GOODBYE. MY HEART WILL FOREVER LONG FOR YOUR LOVE, YOUR TOUCH, YOUR LAUGHTER, YOUR SMILE. MAYBE I WAS HOPING THAT IT WOULD JUST BE IF WE COULD LOVE AGAIN—MAYBE NOT WITH EACH OTHER, BUT WITH SOMEONE WHO COULD ONE DAY FILL THE VOID THAT WE ONCE HAD.

IN THE GARDEN OF EDEN, YOU WERE MY ADAM, AND I WAS YOUR EVE. UNTIL THAT DAY I ALLOWED THE DEVIL TO TRICK ME INTO EATING THE UNFORBIDDEN FRUIT, CAUSING US BOTH TO SIN. SO NOW YOU BLAME ME FOR WHAT WE BOTH DID. I WILL LEAVE YOU ALONE IN THE GARDEN OF EDEN TO SEARCH YOUR SOUL AND FIND OUT HOW TO LOVE YOURSELF. HOW MUST I LET GO OF THE ONE TRUE LOVE THAT I FOUND? I MUST LET GO AND GIVE IT TO GOD, FOR GOD ALONE CAN HEAL MY BROKEN HEART AND HEAL YOURS TOO. SO I SAY GOODBYE TO MY ADAM. I WILL FOREVER HAVE LOVE IN MY HEART FOR YOU, ADAM; LOVE ALWAYS, EVE.

A LOVE STORY OF TWO PEOPLE WHO LOVED EACH OTHER SO MUCH THAT THEY HURT ONE ANOTHER BECAUSE NEITHER WANTED TO TELL THE OTHER HOW THEY TRULY CARED, ALLOWING LIES TO ROB THEM OF THEIR ONE TRUE LOVE—THE LOVE THEY HAD FOR EACH OTHER. DON'T ALLOW THE DEVIL TO STEAL, KILL, AND DESTROY YOUR LOVE FOR FAMILY OR THE LOVE YOU HAVE FOR THAT SPECIAL SOMEONE IN YOUR LIFE. DON'T LET THE DEVIL WIN. TRUST GOD, FOR GOD IS ALL THE LOVE YOU NEED. WAIT ON GOD TO SEND YOU SOMEONE INTO YOUR LIFE. GOD SENDS US WHAT WE NEED, NOT ALWAYS WHAT WE WANT, BUT GOD WILL GIVE US THE DESIRES OF OUR HEARTS. LET US ALLOW GOD TO MEET OUR NEEDS.

CHAPTER 1:

THE SOUL OF A MAN

WHAT DOES GOD SAY ABOUT OUR SOUL IN THE BIBLE? GENESIS 2:7

GOD DID NOT MAKE A BODY AND PUT A SOUL INTO IT. GOD FORMED A MAN'S BODY FROM THE DUST, THEN HE BREATHED A DIVINE BREATH INTO MAN. GOD BREATHED HIS SPIRIT INTO MAN.

HOW DOES THE SOUL WORK?

THE SOUL ACTS AS A LINK BETWEEN THE MATERIAL BODY AND THE SPIRITUAL SELF AND THEREFORE SHARES SOME CHARACTERISTICS OF THE BODY. THE SOUL CAN BE ATTRACTED EITHER TOWARD THE SPIRITUAL REALM OR THE NATURAL REALM, SO YOUR SOUL BATTLES WITH GOOD AND EVIL. ACCORDING TO THE HEBREW WORD NEPHESH, WHICH WAS TRANSLATED IN SOME ENGLISH BIBLES AS "SOUL," THE MEANING IS "A LIVING BEING." IN THE SEPTUAGINT, THE GREEK WORD MEANING "SOUL" WAS USED. THE NEW TESTAMENT ALSO USES THE HEBREW MEANING RATHER THAN

THE GREEK. THE ONLY HEBREW WORD TRANSLATED AS "SOUL" IN THE ENGLISH BIBLE, NEPHESH, REFERS TO A LIVING, BREATHING, CONSCIOUS BODY RATHER THAN A MORTAL SOUL, MAINTAINING THE SAME MEANING AS THE HEBREW, WITHOUT REFERENCE TO THE NEW TESTAMENT. THE GREEK WORD TRANSLATED AS "SOUL," PSYCHE, HAS THE SAME MEANING AS THE HEBREW WORD BUT WITHOUT REFERENCE TO AN IMMORTAL SOUL.

MY SOUL HAS BEEN ABUSED. WE CAME INTO THIS WORLD WITH A BODY, SPIRIT, AND SOUL. WE MUST UNDERSTAND HOW TO CONNECT WITH GOD SPIRITUALLY. OUR SOUL IS BASICALLY WHO WE ARE—OUR MIND, OUR EMOTIONS, AND OUR WILL. THE FUNCTION OF OUR SOUL IS TO EXPRESS OURSELVES TO GOD. SOME OF OUR THOUGHTS ARE OUR OWN, AND SOME ARE GOD'S THOUGHTS, BUT WE MUST REPENT AND INVITE GOD INTO OUR LIVES. WE MUST CONTINUE TO PRAY FOR OUR MINDS BECAUSE THERE IS A WAR GOING ON IN THE MIND. GOD WANTS OUR MINDS, AND THE DEVIL WANTS OUR MINDS. THIS INVISIBLE WAR REFERS TO THE SOUL AND MIND.

THE SPIRITUAL REALM

(EPHESIANS 6:12, HEBREWS 11:3)

WHAT IS REQUIRED OF US TO BELIEVE? WE MUST BELIEVE IN THE PHYSICAL REALM IN ORDER TO BE WELCOMED INTO GOD'S SPIRITUAL REALM. THERE ARE SOME PEOPLE WHO ARE ABLE TO SEE WITH THEIR PHYSICAL EYES INTO THE SPIRITUAL REALM. (DANIEL 10:7-11 AND 2 KINGS 6:11-17) THE INVISIBLE REALM ALLOWS THE ANGELS TO BRIDGE THE GAPS IN THE PHYSICAL REALM AND SEE INTO THE SPIRITUAL REALM. GOD OPENED THE EYES OF ELISHA'S SERVANT TO SEE THE HOST OF GOD'S ARMY. HIS SPIRITUAL EYES WERE OPENED TO SEE THE SPIRITUAL WARFARE AROUND HIM, WHILE EVERYONE ELSE FELT THE TERROR AND FLED. DANIEL WAS GRANTED ACCESS TO SEE, HEAR, AND SPEAK SPIRITUALLY AS HE COMMUNICATED WITH THE ANGELS IN THE PHYSICAL REALM.

IN THE NATURAL REALM, THE WAY MAN IS ABLE TO WORSHIP AND COMMUNICATE WITH GOD IS THROUGH THE SOUL. THE SOUL IS THE MEETING PLACE WHERE THE BODY AND THE SPIRIT CONNECT WITH GOD'S SPIRIT IN THE SPIRITUAL REALM. THE SPIRIT CONTROLS THE BODY, AND THE SOUL IS IN

BETWEEN THE TWO. THE SOUL BINDS THE SPIRIT AND THE BODY TOGETHER AS ONE. THE SPIRIT CAN CONTROL THE BODY THROUGH THE SOUL, CAUSING IT TO SUBMIT TO GOD. THE BRAIN AND THE HEART'S FUNCTIONS COME FROM THE SOUL. THE BODY AND THE SOUL ARE CONTROLLED BY THE SPIRIT OF GOD.

THE SOUL IS SLIGHTLY DIFFERENT FROM THE BODY. THE SOUL CONTAINS THE TRUE SPIRITUAL MIND, AND THIS IS WHERE WE MUST GUARD OUR HEARTS AND SOULS EMOTIONALLY AND SPIRITUALLY. THE DEVIL CAN ENTER OUR HEARTS AND SOULS IF WE HOLD ONTO UNFORGIVENESS. UNFORGIVENESS IN OUR HEARTS WILL LEAVE A DOOR OPEN FOR THE ENEMY TO ENTER. THESE UNCLEAN SPIRITS WILL TRY TO ENTER THE BODY TO WEAKEN THE SPIRIT, WHICH WILL ALSO WEAKEN A PERSON'S FAITH. THIS CAN LEAD TO PHYSICAL ILLNESS ENTERING THE BODY, BUT WE MUST NOT GIVE IN TO THESE EVIL THOUGHTS THAT THE DEVIL TRIES TO PUT IN OUR MINDS. WE MUST CONTINUE TO READ GOD'S WORD SO IT MAY BE HIDDEN IN OUR HEARTS. WE MUST CONTINUE TO PRAY SO THAT GOD WILL PROTECT OUR MINDS, SO THE HEART AND SOUL CAN HEAL.

"IF WE FOLLOW THE HOLY SPIRIT, IT WILL LEAD US INTO ETERNAL LIFE." [THE TRUE SPIRIT OF GOD]

CHAPTER 2:

THE DIFFERENT BETWEEN BODY, SPIRIT, AND SOUL

THE BODY IS THE HOUSE THAT HOLDS THE SPIRIT AND THE SOUL. THERE IS A DIFFERENCE BETWEEN THE SOUL, THE SPIRIT, AND THE BODY. 1 THESSALONIANS 5:23:

"NOW MAY THE GOD OF PEACE MAKE YOU HOLY IN EVERY WAY, AND MAY YOUR SPIRIT AND SOUL AND BODY BE KEPT BLAMELESS UNTIL OUR LORD JESUS CHRIST COMES AGAIN."

THERE ARE THREE PARTS OF THE TEMPLE: THE SPIRIT, THE SOUL, AND THE BODY. GENESIS 2:7:

"THEN THE LORD GOD FORMED MAN FROM THE DUST OF THE GROUND; THEN HE BREATHED THE BREATH OF LIFE INTO MAN'S NOSTRILS, AND THE MAN BECAME A LIVING BEING."

HEBREWS 4:12:

"FOR THE WORD OF GOD IS ALIVE AND POWERFUL. IT IS SHARPER THAN A TWO-EDGED SWORD, CUTTING BETWEEN SOUL AND SPIRIT, BETWEEN JOINT AND MARROW; IT EXPOSES

OUR INNERMOST THOUGHTS AND DESIRES."

IN THE BOOK OF HEBREWS, WE SEE THAT THE SPIRIT AND THE SOUL NEED TO BE DIVIDED FROM ONE ANOTHER. THE WORD OF GOD IS LIVING AND OPERATING, SHARPER THAN A TWO-EDGED SWORD, PIERCING EVEN TO THE DIVIDING OF THE SOUL AND THE SPIRIT, AND OF JOINT AND MARROW, ABLE TO DISCERN THE THOUGHTS AND INTENTIONS OF THE HEART. THERE IS A NEED TO DIVIDE THE SPIRIT FROM THE SOUL AND THE SOUL FROM THE SPIRIT.

THE BOOK OF HEBREWS BEGINS TO SPEAK OF CHRIST JESUS, THE HIGH PRIEST. WHEN THE HIGH PRIEST OFFERED UP A SACRIFICE TO GOD, HE ALWAYS USED INSTRUMENTS. WE ARE GOD'S SACRIFICE TO GOD, AND JESUS CHRIST IS THE HIGH PRIEST, WITH THE HOLY SPIRIT DIVIDING OUR SOUL FROM OUR SPIRIT BY THE WORD OF GOD. THE BODY, SOUL, AND SPIRIT REFLECT THE TRINITY, WHICH IS THREE IN ONE.

THE HOLY SPIRIT WILL SHOW US IN GOD'S WORD WHAT IS OF OUR SOUL AND WHAT IS OF OUR SPIRIT. GOD'S WORD WILL ALWAYS GUIDE AND LEAD US. THE HOLY SPIRIT WILL ALWAYS REVEAL TO US THE DIFFERENCE BETWEEN THE SPIRIT AND

THE SOUL. THERE IS A DIFFERENCE BETWEEN THE SPIRIT AND THE SOUL, AND UNDERSTANDING THIS DIFFERENCE IS CRUCIAL.

1 CORINTHIANS 2:9-12:

"FOR IT IS WRITTEN: 'EYES HAVE NOT SEEN, NOR EARS HEARD, NOR HAVE ENTERED INTO THE HEART OF MAN THE THINGS WHICH GOD HAS PREPARED FOR THOSE WHO LOVE HIM.' BUT GOD HAS REVEALED THEM TO US THROUGH HIS SPIRIT. FOR THE SPIRIT SEARCHES ALL THINGS, YES, THE DEEP THINGS OF GOD. FOR WHAT MAN KNOWS THE THINGS OF A MAN EXCEPT THE SPIRIT OF THE MAN WHICH IS IN HIM? EVEN SO, NO ONE KNOWS THE THINGS OF GOD EXCEPT THE SPIRIT OF GOD. NOW WE HAVE RECEIVED, NOT THE SPIRIT OF THE WORLD, BUT THE SPIRIT WHO IS FROM GOD, THAT WE MIGHT KNOW THE THINGS THAT HAVE BEEN FREELY GIVEN TO US BY GOD. THESE THINGS WE ALSO SPEAK, NOT IN WORDS WHICH MAN'S WISDOM TEACHES, BUT WHICH THE HOLY SPIRIT TEACHES, COMPARING SPIRITUAL THINGS WITH SPIRITUAL. BUT THE NATURAL MAN DOES NOT RECEIVE THE THINGS OF THE SPIRIT OF GOD, FOR THEY ARE FOOLISHNESS TO HIM; NOR CAN HE KNOW THEM

BECAUSE THEY ARE SPIRITUALLY DISCERNED."

GOD'S WORD IS SO POWERFUL AND ABLE TO DISCERN THE DIFFERENCE BETWEEN THE SPIRIT AND THE SOUL. 1 THESSALONIANS 5:23 TELLS US THAT TO UNDERSTAND THE TRUTH ABOUT MANKIND, WE MUST RECOGNIZE THAT THE BODY IS MADE UP OF THREE PARTS: THE SPIRIT, THE SOUL, AND THE BODY. THE SPIRIT IS YOUR LIFELINE TO GOD, YOUR SOUL IS A PART OF YOUR PERSONALITY, YOUR ATTITUDE, AND YOUR THOUGHTS, AND THE BODY IS LIKE A VESSEL THAT HOUSES THE SPIRIT AND THE SOUL. THESE THREE PARTS MAKE UP THE HUMAN BODY, WHICH IS FLESH AND BLOOD. WITHOUT ALL THREE, THE BODY CANNOT LIVE OR HAVE LIFE.

GOD LOOKS INTO OUR SPIRIT. OUR SPIRIT IS WHO WE REALLY ARE TO GOD.

CHAPTER 3:

THE SOUL HAS BEEN ABUSED

WHEN YOUR SOUL HAS BEEN WOUNDED AND YOUR HEART HURTS FROM ALL THE PAIN THAT YOU HAVE BEEN THROUGH IN LIFE, IT LEAVES A HOLE IN THE SOUL. THE ONLY WAY THAT A PERSON CAN BE HEALED IS BY ALIGNING THEIR SPIRIT WITH GOD'S WORD, GIVING GOD YOUR LIFE, REPENTING, AND ALLOWING GOD TO HEAL YOU. A PERSON'S SOUL WILL NEED MENDING, AND OFTEN GOD WILL SEND SOMEONE INTO YOUR LIFE TO HELP YOU HEAL.

THIS HAPPENED TO ME. I WAS PHYSICALLY, MENTALLY, AND SEXUALLY ABUSED, WHICH LEFT A HOLE IN MY SOUL WITH WOUNDS SO DEEP THAT MY HEART NEVER WANTED TO LOVE AGAIN. BUT THEN, SOME YEARS AGO, I MET THE MOST AMAZING MAN WHO CAME INTO MY LIFE WHEN I WAS SEEKING GOD, PRAYING AND SAYING I WOULD NEVER GIVE MY HEART TO ANYONE ELSE BECAUSE I JUST DIDN'T WANT TO FEEL THE PAIN THAT MY HEART WAS EXPERIENCING. MY HEART WAS SHATTERING INTO MILLIONS OF PIECES, AND I SHUT MYSELF OFF FROM PEOPLE, RETREATING INTO A SHELL

ALONE. MY SPIRIT AND SOUL BEGAN TO BATTLE UNTIL GOD'S ANGEL OF LOVE CAME INTO MY LIFE AND TOUCHED ME.

HE BROUGHT ME OUT OF THE SHELL I HAD CRAWLED INTO, PRAYING TO GOD, SAYING I WAS DONE WITH RELATIONSHIPS AND JUST WANTED TO SERVE HIM WITHOUT EVER THINKING ABOUT LOVE OR A RELATIONSHIP WITH A MAN. I WAS DONE, BUT GOD DIDN'T WANT ME TO STAY BROKEN AND LEFT WITH A HOLE IN MY SOUL, AND MY HEART WAS ALSO IN MILLIONS OF PIECES UNTIL MY LOVE AGENT, YES, AN ANGEL OF LOVE, CAME INTO MY LIFE.

THIS AMAZING MAN AND I CONNECTED SPIRITUALLY, AND I BEGAN TO COME OUT OF MY SHELL BECAUSE OF HIM. HE TOLD ME THAT IT WASN'T LOVE THAT HURT ME; IT WAS THE PERSON TO WHOM I GAVE MY LOVE THAT CAUSED THE PAIN. HE BEGAN TO TEACH ME ABOUT LOVE AND HOW TO LOVE. HE SAID IF YOU ALLOW THINGS TO HAPPEN NATURALLY, YOU WILL FIND TRUE LOVE. MY HEART BEGAN TO MEND AS IT SEEMED THAT ALL THOSE SHATTERED PIECES WERE COMING BACK TOGETHER. THE DEEP CUTS AND WOUNDS BEGAN TO HEAL, AND I STARTED TO SMILE AGAIN AS GOD BEGAN TO HEAL MY HEART

AND SOUL, AND MY SPIRIT BEGAN TO COME ALIVE.

GOD IS LOVE, AND WE MUST LEARN TO LOVE ONE ANOTHER.

GOD IS LOVE, AND WE MUST TRUST HIS PLANS FOR OUR LIVES.

GOD SAID IN HIS WORD THAT HE WILL BE EVERYTHING WE NEED HIM TO BE IN OUR LIVES IF WE JUST TRUST HIM AND ALLOW HIM TO LEAD AND GUIDE US. WE MUST ALLOW GOD INTO OUR LIVES COMPLETELY.

THIS STORY THAT I'M WRITING IS TRUE. I'M WRITING IT BECAUSE IT SERVES AS AN EXAMPLE OF HOW GOD ALLOWED SOMEONE TO COME INTO A PERSON'S LIFE AND HELP THEM HEAL. BUT THEN THE DEVIL TRIED TO PUT DOUBT IN MY MIND BECAUSE I HAD SOMEONE IN MY LIFE ENCOURAGING ME AND HELPING ME TO BELIEVE IN LOVE AND MYSELF AGAIN. I FELL IN LOVE SO NATURALLY WITH THIS MAN, AND THE DEVIL TRIED TO PUT NEGATIVE THOUGHTS IN MY MIND: "YOU ARE ALL ALONE, NO ONE LOVES YOU." I WANTED TO GO BACK INTO THE SHELL I HAD ONCE COME OUT OF.

BUT I FOUGHT HARD NOT TO GO BACK. I COULDN'T GO BACKWARDS, SO I BEGAN TO BATTLE ONCE AGAIN, BUT THIS TIME WITH MY HEART, SOUL, AND MIND, STRUGGLING WITH

THE FEAR OF BEING IN LOVE WITH SOMEONE SO LOVING, CARING, AND PATIENT. I WANTED TO RUN, AND FEAR BEGAN TO SET IN AS I FELT THAT IF I LOVED HIM, I MIGHT LOSE THE RELATIONSHIP WITH HIM. I DIDN'T WANT TO LOSE THE ONE PERSON WHO WAS THERE FOR ME.

THEN I BEGAN TO FIGHT MY FEELINGS. I DIDN'T WANT TO HAVE THESE FEELINGS. I DIDN'T WANT TO BE IN LOVE WITH THIS PERSON THAT GOD HAD PLACED IN MY LIFE TO HELP ME MEND. I WAS CONFUSED BECAUSE I WANTED TO RUN AND HIDE, BUT GOD IS NOT THE AUTHOR OF CONFUSION. SO NOW I WAS BATTLING WITH MY HEART WHILE MY HEART WAS TRYING TO MEND, AND MY MIND WAS FULL OF FEAR. BUT GOD DID NOT GIVE US THE SPIRIT OF FEAR.

I BEGAN TO PRAY FOR GOD TO TAKE CONTROL OF MY MIND BECAUSE THE DEVIL WANTED TO CONFUSE ME TO KEEP ME FROM MY CALLING AND DESTINY. I FOUGHT MY BATTLES ON MY KNEES, PRAYING AND ASKING GOD TO FIGHT MY BATTLES FOR ME AND GIVE ME STRENGTH, FOR ALL OUR BATTLES BELONG TO GOD. I ALLOWED GOD TO RESTORE ME PHYSICALLY, MENTALLY, EMOTIONALLY, AND SEXUALLY,

AND GOD ALSO HEALED ME SPIRITUALLY.

NOW I KNOW I DIDN'T WANT TO QUENCH THE HOLY SPIRIT. THE HOLY SPIRIT NEEDS TO OPERATE IN A PERSON'S LIFE; WE MUST LISTEN AND ALLOW OUR SPIRIT TO CONNECT WITH GOD'S SPIRIT. WE MUST NOT ALLOW OUR SOUL TO REMAIN ABUSED.

CHAPTER 4:

STRONGHOLDS IN THE SOUL{HEART}

OUR HEART AND EMOTIONS ARE OUR SOUL, STRONGHOLDS THAT ARE IN THE HEART AND SOUL. THE HEART MUST ALSO HEAL. THE HEART IS IN BETWEEN THE SPIRIT AND THE SOUL. A PERSON MUST NOT HOLD HURT IN THEIR HEART. ONE MUST NOT HOLD UNFORGIVENESS, BITTERNESS, OR ANGER IN THE HEART, BECAUSE IT WILL CAUSE THE HEART TO BECOME COLD AND DARK LIKE THE DEVIL. SO ONE MUST LET GO OF ALL OF THESE THINGS BY ASKING GOD TO CLEANSE THE HEART AND GIVE A PERSON A NEW AND CLEAN HEART. ONCE THE HEART IS HEALED, YOUR SOUL CAN BEGIN TO HEAL.

OUR BODY IS A TEMPLE, A HOUSE FOR OUR SPIRIT AND SOUL. OUR SOUL IS WHO WE ARE; THE BIBLE SPEAKS OF THE SOUL AS THE HEART OF THE BODY. THE SOUL IS UNIQUE, AND OUR SPIRIT IS THE PART OF THE BODY THAT ALLOWS US TO COMMUNICATE WITH GOD. WHAT CAUSES THE WOUNDS OF THE SOUL? THESE ARE THE THINGS THAT COULD CAUSE WOUNDS IN THE SOUL: ABANDONMENT, REJECTION, BETRAYAL, HUMILIATION, AND INJUSTICE. A WOUNDED SOUL

WILL ALWAYS BE A PART OF A PERSON AS LONG AS THEY HOLD ONTO THE PAIN. SOME PEOPLE MIGHT THINK THAT HOLDING ON TO THESE WOUNDS AND PAIN MIGHT PROTECT THEM, BUT THAT IS NOT TRUE. THE LONGER A PERSON HOLDS ON TO THIS KIND OF PAIN, THE MORE IT WILL BECOME STRONGHOLDS IN THEIR LIFE. A PERSON MUST PRAY AND ASK GOD TO BREAK AND REMOVE THESE STRONGHOLDS FROM THEIR LIVES BY REPENTING, OR IT WILL ALLOW THE DEVIL TO HAVE ACCESS TO CONTROL AND KEEP THESE STRONGHOLDS OVER THEM.

WHEN A PERSON IS HURT EMOTIONALLY, THE PAIN IS SO DEEP THEY CAN BECOME EMOTIONALLY SCARRED. EMOTIONAL SCARS DO NOT HEAL RIGHT AWAY, AND SOMETIMES SOMETHING MIGHT TRIGGER THE EMOTIONS, CAUSING THE BEHAVIOR OF THAT PERSON TO CHANGE AND REACT IN A NEGATIVE WAY. WHENEVER SOMETHING HAPPENS THAT TRIGGERS THEM, IT ALLOWS THE DEVIL TO CONTINUE TO HAVE A STRONGHOLD OVER A PERSON'S LIFE. IF A PERSON HARBORS BITTERNESS, ANGER, UNFORGIVENESS, REMORSE, GUILT, DOUBT, AND SELF-IMPOSED EMOTIONS, IT WILL AFFECT THE MIND, CAUSING A PERSON TO HAVE NEGATIVE THOUGHTS

AND ALLOWING THE DEVIL TO TRY TO CONTROL THE PERSON'S MIND. PRAY AND ALLOW GOD'S WORD AND THE HOLY SPIRIT TO HELP HEAL IN JESUS' NAME.

THERE MAY BE SO MANY STRONG EMOTIONS THAT A PERSON MAY NOT KNOW HOW TO PROCESS THEM. EVENTUALLY, THESE FEELINGS ARE EXPRESSED IN SO MANY WAYS. A PERSON MAY NEED TO BE HONEST ABOUT WHAT THEIR PAST HURT IS AND EXPRESS THEIR FEELINGS. A PERSON MUST CONFRONT THE PAIN, GUILT, AND SHAME THAT THEY ARE HOLDING ON TO. UNFORGIVENESS AND ALL THAT HURT MAY BE CONTROLLED BY EXPLOSIVE EMOTIONS THAT ARE STILL HIDDEN IN THE HEART AND SOUL.

PEOPLE CAN BE DESTROYED BY RAPE, SEXUAL ABUSE, OR INCEST. THIS WILL MAKE A PERSON WANT TO RUN AND HIDE. A PERSON MUST MAKE GOD THEIR HIDING PLACE. GOD HEARS OUR CRIES AND WILL HIDE US IN A SECRET PLACE; HE WILL ALWAYS SHIELD AND PROTECT HIS PEOPLE WHO CALL ON HIM AND ASK HIM FOR FORGIVENESS OF OUR SINS. (2 SAMUEL 22:1-33)

POEM: HOW CAN I SAY GOODBYE

HOW CAN I SAY GOODBYE TO YOU, HOW CAN I SAY THAT I STILL LOVE YOU AND SAY GOODBYE TO WHAT I'M FEELING? I CARED ABOUT YOU, BUT I MUST LET YOU GO. HOW CAN I

SAY GOODBYE WHEN MY HEART IS BROKEN AND I STILL LOVE YOU? HOW CAN I SAY GOODBYE TO WHAT WE HAD WHEN IT HURTS SO BAD TO CONTINUE TO HAVE THESE FEELINGS?

WHEN YOU'RE NO LONGER THERE, HOW CAN I SAY GOODBYE WITH TEARS IN MY EYES? I MUST SAY GOODBYE SO MY HEART CAN BE HEALED AND MY SOUL NO LONGER HURTS, SO NOW I'M

SAYING GOODBYE.

SOMETIMES WE MUST LET GO AND SAY GOODBYE IN ORDER FOR OUR SOUL TO BE HEALED BY GOD. GOD WILL ALSO MOVE PEOPLE OUT OF OUR LIVES BECAUSE HE KNOWS WHAT'S BEST

FOR US. GOD DEALS WITH YOUR SPIRIT, NOT YOUR FLESHLY BODY; THE SPIRIT AND THE SOUL WORK TO CONTROL THE BODY.

CHAPTER 5:

WAR IN THE MIND

THERE IS A WAR GOING ON IN THE MIND. GOD WANTS OUR MIND, AND THE DEVIL WANTS OUR MIND. THIS INVISIBLE WAR REFERS TO THE SOUL AND THE MIND. THE SOUL'S WOUNDS ARE A RESULT OF SIN. MOST SINS ARE COMMITTED AGAINST A PERSON, AND THE SOUL IS WOUNDED AND ABUSED SO BADLY THAT A PERSON BECOMES EMOTIONALLY SCARRED. IT'S NOTHING LIKE A SCAR YOU RECEIVE ON YOUR SKIN. THE SCAR ON THE SKIN LEAVES A VISIBLE SCAR, BUT EMOTIONAL SCARS REMAIN DEEP IN A PERSON'S HEART THAT HASN'T BEEN HEALED.

IF YOU ARE EMOTIONALLY SCARRED, ONCE SOMETHING HAPPENS, IT SOMETIMES TRIGGERS EMOTIONS IN A PERSON WHO IS ALREADY DEEPLY WOUNDED. THE SOUL IS WOUNDED AND NEEDS HEALING. IF NOT ADDRESSED, THE DEVIL WILL CONTINUE TO HAVE A STRONGHOLD IN A PERSON'S LIFE. REMEMBER, THE DEVIL AND HIS DEMONS NEED A BODY TO USE, SO THEY MUST TRY TO FIND A WAY INTO YOUR SOUL, AND THE DEVIL USES THE MIND AND HEART AS A WAY IN.

BECAUSE OF SINS, PEOPLE HOLD ONTO PAST HURT, WHICH CAUSES OUR SOULS TO BE ABUSED AND SCARRED.

THE MIND HAS THE BASIC FUNCTIONS OF THINKING, FEELING, AND DESIRING. THESE THREE FUNCTIONS OF THE MIND - THOUGHTS, FEELINGS, AND DESIRES - CAN BE GUIDED OR DIRECTED EITHER BY ONE'S POTENTIAL OR TENDENCIES TO FUNCTION AUTOMATICALLY AND UNCONSCIOUSLY.

WHAT EMOTIONAL WOUNDS DOES A PERSON SUFFER? THE SOUL CAN HARBOR BITTERNESS, ANGER, UNFORGIVENESS, REMORSE, GUILT, AND ABANDONMENT. BY HOLDING ON TO THESE EMOTIONS, THEY WILL BECOME BURIED DEEP DOWN IN A PERSON'S MIND AND HEART, ALLOWING THESE THINGS TO BECOME EMBEDDED INTO A PERSON'S CONSCIOUS AND UNCONSCIOUS MIND.

LET'S TALK ABOUT THE CONSCIOUS AND UNCONSCIOUS MIND. THE CONSCIOUS MIND CONTAINS ALL OF THE THOUGHTS, MEMORIES, AND FEELINGS OF WHICH A PERSON IS AWARE AT ANY GIVEN MOMENT. THE UNCONSCIOUS MIND IS A RESERVOIR OF FEELINGS, THOUGHTS, AND MEMORIES THAT ARE OUTSIDE OF A PERSON'S CONSCIOUS AWARENESS.

SIGMUND FREUD WAS THE FOUNDER OF PSYCHOANALYSIS, A METHOD FOR TREATING MENTAL ILLNESS. FREUD'S THEORIES OF THE CONSCIOUS MIND AND UNCONSCIOUS MIND ARE USED TO DEVELOP HIS THEORIES, WHICH REFER TO MYTHOLOGY. FREUD DIVIDED THE MIND INTO LEVELS, EACH WITH THEIR OWN ROLES AND FUNCTIONS.

THE PRECONSCIOUS CONSISTS OF ANYTHING THAT COULD POTENTIALLY BE BROUGHT INTO THE CONSCIOUS MIND. THE CONSCIOUS MIND CONTAINS ALL OF THE THOUGHTS, MEMORIES, AND FEELINGS OF WHICH WE ARE AWARE, AND THIS IS THE ASPECT OF OUR MENTAL PROCESSING THAT WE CAN THINK AND TALK ABOUT RATIONALLY. THIS ALSO INCLUDES OUR MEMORY, WHICH IS NOT ALWAYS A PART OF CONSCIOUSNESS BUT CAN BE RETRIEVED EASILY AND BROUGHT INTO AWARENESS.

THE UNCONSCIOUS MIND IS A RESERVOIR OF FEELINGS, THOUGHTS, URGES, AND MEMORIES THAT ARE OUTSIDE OF OUR CONSCIOUS AWARENESS. THE UNCONSCIOUS MIND CONTAINS CONTENTS THAT ARE UNACCEPTABLE OR UNPLEASANT, SUCH AS FEELINGS OF PAIN, ANXIETY, OR

CONFLICT. ACCORDING TO FREUD, THOUGHTS AND EMOTIONS OUTSIDE OF OUR AWARENESS CONTINUE TO INFLUENCE OUR BEHAVIORS, EVEN THOUGH A PERSON CAN BE UNAWARE OR UNCONSCIOUS OF THE UNDERLYING INFLUENCES. THE UNCONSCIOUS MIND CAN REPRESS FEELINGS, HIDDEN MEMORIES, HABITS, THOUGHTS, AND EMOTIONS THAT ARE TOO PAINFUL, EMBARRASSING, SHAMEFUL, OR DISTRESSING TO CONSCIOUSLY FACE AND ARE STORED IN THE RESERVOIR THAT MAKES UP THE UNCONSCIOUS MIND.

THE PRECONSCIOUS MIND CONTAINS ALL OF THE THINGS THAT A PERSON COULD POTENTIALLY PULL INTO CONSCIOUS AWARENESS. THE PRECONSCIOUS MIND CAN ALSO ACT AS A GUARD, CONTROLLING THE INFORMATION THAT IS ALLOWED TO ENTER INTO THE CONSCIOUS MIND. FREUD'S IDEAS HAVE BECOME VERY IMPORTANT CONTRIBUTIONS TO PSYCHOLOGY.

PSYCHOANALYTIC THERAPY, WHICH EXPLORES HOW THE UNCONSCIOUS MIND INFLUENCES BEHAVIOR AND THOUGHTS, HAS BECOME AN IMPORTANT TOOL IN THE TREATMENT OF MENTAL ILLNESS. SIGMUND FREUD DIVIDED HUMAN CONSCIOUSNESS INTO THREE LEVELS OF AWARENESS: THE

CONSCIOUS, THE PRECONSCIOUS, AND THE UNCONSCIOUS.

WE MUST TRY TO UNDERSTAND OUR CONSCIOUS, UNCONSCIOUS, AND PRECONSCIOUS MINDS SO WE CAN DEAL WITH OUR FEELINGS AND EMOTIONS. FEEL FREE TO READ MORE ABOUT SIGMUND FREUD'S THEORIES, AS THEY ARE VERY INTERESTING TO RESEARCH.

CHAPTER 6:

SOUL RAPE, THE RAPING OF THE SOUL

THE RAPING OF THE SOUL - THE ACT OF FORCING SOMEONE TO WITNESS AN EVENT THAT CAUSES A PERSON'S SOUL TO SPIRAL INTO DEPRESSION AND SUICIDAL THOUGHTS, LEADING THEM TO DIE INSIDE. THESE DEEP WOUNDS WILL BECOME DEEPLY ROOTED. A CHILD WHO LOSES THEIR INNOCENCE WILL STRUGGLE WITH TRUST, OR THEY WILL BEGIN TO ACT OUT EMOTIONALLY. THEIR BEHAVIOR BEGINS TO CHANGE WHEN CONFRONTED OR REMINDED OF THE PAIN AND ABUSE THEY DO NOT KNOW HOW TO HANDLE.

"GOD DEALS WITH YOUR SPIRIT, NOT YOUR FLESHLY BODY." THE SPIRIT AND THE SOUL WORK TOGETHER TO CONTROL THE BODY.

TRUST BECOMES AN ISSUE WHEN A PERSON IS ABUSED BY PEOPLE THEY LOVE OR RESPECT. THE WOUNDS BECOME SO DEEP WITHIN THEIR SOUL THAT IT IS CALLED SOUL RAPE.

SOUL RAPE WILL CAUSE A PERSON TO STRUGGLE WITH SELF-HATRED OR SELF-LOATHING. THIS CAN LEAD TO A DEEP

DISLIKE OR HATRED FOR THEMSELVES, AND THEY MAY ALSO BECOME ANGRY WITH THEMSELVES. SOUL RAPE CAN ALSO CAUSE A PERSON TO HARBOR HATRED FOR FAMILY OR OTHERS.

SELF-HATRED WILL CAUSE A PERSON TO DO TWO THINGS:

BLAME OTHERS WHO HAVE SHAMED THEM, LEADING TO JUDGMENT IN THEIR MIND AND SPIRIT.

DEVELOP DEEP WOUNDS IN THE SOUL, WHICH CAUSES FURTHER ABUSE AND LEAVES A HOLE IN THE SOUL.

EMOTIONAL RAPE IS THE USE OF A PERSON'S EMOTIONS, SUCH AS LOVE, WITHOUT CONSENT. THIS CAN BE VERY DAMAGING TO THE SOUL AND SPIRIT. THIS IS WHERE TRUST ISSUES BEGIN, AND THE PERSON MAY FEEL THEY CAN NEVER TRUST OR LOVE AGAIN.

SEXUAL RAPE IS A VIOLATION OF A PERSON'S BODY.

EMOTIONAL RAPE IS A VIOLATION OF THE HUMAN SOUL THAT LEADS TO TRUST ISSUES.

SPIRITUAL RAPE IS THE VIOLENT AND SEXUAL INVASION OF THE HUMAN SPIRIT, THE NATURAL BODY, AND THE SPIRITUAL

BODY.

SPIRITUAL RAPE VIOLATES THE SOUL, LEAVING A PERSON BROKENHEARTED AND WITH A BROKEN SPIRIT.

GOD HEALS THE BROKENHEARTED AND BINDS UP THEIR WOUNDS. (PSALMS 147:3)

THREE WAYS GOD, THE TRINITY.

GOD UNDERSTANDS OUR PAIN. (ROMANS 8:26)

JESUS UNDERSTANDS OUR WEAKNESS. (HEBREWS 4:1-5)

THE HOLY SPIRIT UNDERSTANDS OUR FEELINGS AND EMOTIONS. (PSALMS 33:5)

WE HAVE EMOTIONS BECAUSE WE ARE MADE IN THE IMAGE OF GOD. JESUS UNDERSTANDS OUR PAIN; HE ALSO SUFFERED THE SAME PAIN THE WORLD HAS SUFFERED. HE WAS BETRAYED, ABANDONED, AND FATIGUED. HE CAME INTO THIS WORLD AND LIVED AS A HUMAN. JESUS HAS EXPERIENCED EVERY PAIN WE HAVE EXPERIENCED AS HUMAN BEINGS. HE IS OUR HIGH PRIEST.

THEN THERE IS THE HOLY SPIRIT. WHEN WE GET TIRED OF WAITING FOR OUR PRAYERS TO BE ANSWERED AND DON'T

KNOW WHAT TO PRAY FOR, THE HOLY SPIRIT PRAYS FOR US. THE BIBLE SAYS THAT WHEN WE ARE IN PAIN, THE HOLY SPIRIT MAKES PRAYERS FOR US, TURNING OUR WORDLESS, ACHING TEARS AND PAIN INTO PRAYERS. THE HOLY SPIRIT KNOWS OUR FEELINGS, AND IF YOUR SOUL HURTS, YOU DON'T HAVE TO GO THROUGH THE PAIN ALONE. JESUS SAID HE WOULD LEAVE US A COMFORTER, THE HOLY SPIRIT, TO INTERCEDE ON OUR BEHALF. THE SPIRIT OF TRUTH, THE HOLY SPIRIT. (JOHN 14:9)

GOD WILL TAKE ALL THE BROKEN PIECES OF A PERSON'S LIFE AND PUT THEM BACK TOGETHER AGAIN. GOD WILL NEVER LEAVE US ALONE TO DEAL WITH OUR PAIN, BUT WE MUST GIVE IT TO HIM. WE MUST ALLOW GOD TO MEET OUR SPIRITUAL NEEDS.

IT TAKES TIME FOR A PERSON'S SOUL TO HEAL WHEN THEY HAVE DEEP WOUNDS AND THEIR SOUL HAS BEEN ABUSED. ONE MUST ALLOW GOD TO HEAL THEM PHYSICALLY, EMOTIONALLY, SPIRITUALLY, AND SOMETIMES SEXUALLY. WE MUST ALLOW GOD TO RESTORE US FROM ALL PAST HURT BEFORE WE CAN TRULY BE HEALED AND MOVE FORWARD IN LIFE. ONCE HEALED, A PERSON WILL NO LONGER BE

PSYCHOLOGICALLY BOUND IN THEIR SOUL, SPIRIT, AND MIND.

PLEASE ALLOW GOD TO HEAL THE HOLE IN YOUR SOUL. ONCE THE SOUL IS HEALED FROM ALL THE PAIN, THE WOUNDS WILL BEGIN TO HEAL, AND YOU WILL BE FREE TO LIVE AND LOVE AGAIN. I'M FREE, AND IT FEELS GOOD.

CHAPTER 7:

ENERGY THAT FLOWS IN THE BODY - THE SEVEN MAIN CHAKRAS

THE HUMAN BODY CONSISTS OF ENERGY THAT VIBRATES SLOWLY THROUGHOUT THE BODY. CHAKRAS, WHICH MEANS "WHEEL," REFER TO ENERGY POINTS WITHIN YOUR BODY. THEY ARE THOUGHT TO BE SPINNING DISKS OF ENERGY THAT SHOULD STAY OPEN AND ALIGNED, AS THEY CORRESPOND TO BUNDLES OF NERVES OR ORGANS WITHIN OUR ENERGETIC BODY, AFFECTING OUR EMOTIONAL AND PHYSICAL WELL-BEING.

THERE ARE SEVEN MAIN ENERGY CENTERS IN THE BODY, KNOWN AS CHAKRAS. EACH CHAKRA IS LOCATED THROUGHOUT THE BODY, CORRELATING TO SPECIFIC PARTS OF THE BODY THAT CAN MANIFEST PHYSICAL AILMENTS OR DYSFUNCTIONS. THESE ENERGY CENTERS ALSO HOUSE OUR MENTAL AND EMOTIONAL STRENGTHS. THE SEVEN CHAKRAS ARE THE ENERGY CENTERS THROUGH WHICH ENERGY FLOWS. THE WORD CHAKRA IS DERIVED FROM THE SANSKRIT WORD

MEANING "WHEEL," WHICH IS LITERALLY TRANSLATED FROM HINDI AS "WHEEL OF SPINNING ENERGY." A CHAKRA IS LIKE A WHIRLING WHEEL, A POWERHOUSE OF ENERGY.

THE CHAKRAS REGULATE THE FLOW OF ENERGY THROUGHOUT THE ELECTRICAL NETWORK, OR MERIDIANS, THAT RUN THROUGH THE PHYSICAL BODY. THE BODY'S ELECTRICAL SYSTEM RESEMBLES THE WIRING OF A HOUSE, ALLOWING ELECTRICAL CURRENTS TO BE SENT TO EVERY PART OF THE BODY, READY FOR USE WHEN NEEDED. SOMETIMES, THE CHAKRAS BECOME BLOCKED DUE TO STRESS, AND EMOTIONAL, OR PHYSICAL PROBLEMS. IF THE ENERGY SYSTEM CANNOT FLOW FREELY, THESE PROBLEMS WILL OCCUR. THE CONSEQUENCES OF IRREGULAR ENERGY FLOW MAY RESULT IN PHYSICAL ILLNESS OR DISCOMFORT, SUCH AS THE SENSE OF BEING MENTALLY AND EMOTIONALLY OFF BALANCE.

GOD SHARES IN OUR EMOTIONS. PSALM 33:15 REMINDS US THAT THE HOLY SPIRIT WILL BALANCE OUR LIVES, BUT WE MUST PRAY TO THE COMFORTER, WHOM JESUS LEFT SO THAT IF YOU ARE HURTING, YOU WILL NOT HAVE TO GO THROUGH

IT ALONE (JOHN 14:7).

THE SEVEN MAIN CHAKRAS

1. THE CROWN CHAKRA

COLOR: VIOLET

LOCATION: THE TOP OF THE HEAD

ASSOCIATED WITH: CEREBRAL CORTEX, CENTRAL NERVOUS SYSTEM, AND THE PITUITARY GLAND

THE CROWN CHAKRA IS CONNECTED WITH INFORMATION, UNDERSTANDING, ACCEPTANCE, AND BLISS. IT IS SAID TO BE A PERSON'S SPIRITUAL PLACE OF CONNECTION TO GOD, REPRESENTING DIVINE PURPOSE AND PERSONAL DESTINY. A BLOCKAGE IN THIS CHAKRA CAN MANIFEST AS PSYCHOLOGICAL PROBLEMS.

2. THE THIRD EYE CHAKRA

COLOR: INDIGO (A COMBINATION OF RED AND BLUE)

LOCATION: THE CENTER OF THE FOREHEAD, AT EYE LEVEL OR SLIGHTLY ABOVE

THIS CHAKRA IS USED TO QUESTION THE SPIRITUAL NATURE

OF OUR LIVES. IT REPRESENTS QUESTIONING, PERCEPTION, AND KNOWING. IT IS CONNECTED WITH INNER VISION, INTUITION, WISDOM, AND DREAMS FOR THIS LIFE. RECOLLECTIONS OF OTHER LIFETIMES ARE HELD IN THIS CHAKRA. WHEN THE THIRD EYE IS BLOCKED, IT MAY MANIFEST AS A LACK OF FORESIGHT, MENTAL RIGIDITY, SELECTIVE MEMORY LOSS, OR DEPRESSION.

3. THE THROAT CHAKRA

COLOR: BLUE OR TURQUOISE

LOCATION: THE THROAT

ASSOCIATED WITH: NECK, SHOULDERS, ARMS, HANDS, THYROID, AND PARATHYROID GLANDS

THE THROAT CHAKRA GOVERNS COMMUNICATION, CREATIVITY, SELF-EXPRESSION, AND JUDGMENT. IT IS CONNECTED WITH BOTH INNER AND OUTER HEARING, THE SYNTHESIZING OF IDEALS, AND HEALING. IT ALSO DEALS WITH TRANSFORMATION AND PURIFICATION. A BLOCKAGE CAN RESULT IN CREATIVE BLOCKS, DISHONESTY, OR GENERAL PROBLEMS IN COMMUNICATING NEEDS TO OTHERS.

4. THE HEART CHAKRA

COLOR: GREEN

LOCATION: THE HEART

THE HEART CHAKRA IS THE CENTER OF LOVE, COMPASSION, HARMONY, AND PEACE. THE ASIANS SAY THAT THE HEART IS THE HOUSE OF THE SOUL. THIS CHAKRA IS ASSOCIATED WITH THE LUNGS, HEART, ARMS, HANDS, AND THYMUS GLAND. WE FALL IN LOVE THROUGH OUR HEART CHAKRA. FEELINGS OF UNCONDITIONAL LOVE MOVE THROUGH THE EMOTIONAL CENTER, COMMONLY KNOWN AS THE SOLAR PLEXUS, INTO THE SEXUAL CENTER OR BASE CHAKRA, WHERE STRONG FEELINGS OF ATTRACTION CAN BE RELEASED. WHEN THESE ENERGIES MOVE INTO THE BASE CHAKRA, WE MAY DESIRE TO MARRY OR SETTLE DOWN. BLOCKAGES CAN MANIFEST AS IMMUNE SYSTEM ISSUES, LUNG PROBLEMS, OR HEART PROBLEMS. THEY MAY ALSO CAUSE A LACK OF COMPASSION OR UNPRINCIPLED BEHAVIOR.

5. THE SOLAR PLEXUS CHAKRA

COLOR: YELLOW

LOCATION: A FEW INCHES ABOVE THE NAVEL IN THE SOLAR PLEXUS AREA

ASSOCIATED WITH: DIGESTIVE SYSTEM, MUSCLES, PANCREAS, AND ADRENAL GLANDS

THE SOLAR PLEXUS CHAKRA HOLDS A PERSON'S EMOTIONAL LIFE. FEELINGS OF PERSONAL POWER, LAUGHTER, JOY, AND ANGER ARE ASSOCIATED WITH THIS CHAKRA. SENSITIVITY, AMBITION, AND THE ABILITY TO ACHIEVE ARE VERY STRONG HERE. BLOCKAGES MAY MANIFEST AS ANGER, FRUSTRATION, LACK OF DIRECTION, OR A SENSE OF VICTIMIZATION.

6. THE SACRAL OR NAVEL CHAKRA

COLOR: ORANGE

LOCATION: BETWEEN THE BASE OF THE SPINE AND THE NAVEL

ASSOCIATED WITH: LOWER ABDOMEN, KIDNEYS, BLADDER, CIRCULATORY SYSTEM, GLANDS, AND REPRODUCTIVE ORGANS

THE SACRAL CHAKRA REPRESENTS A PERSON'S DESIRES, PLEASURE, SEXUALITY, PROCREATION, AND CREATIVITY. BLOCKAGES MAY MANIFEST AS EMOTIONAL PROBLEMS, OBSESSIVE BEHAVIOR, COMPULSIVE TENDENCIES, OR SEXUAL GUILT.

7. THE BASE OR ROOT CHAKRA

COLOR: RED

LOCATION: THE PERINEUM, AT THE BASE OF THE SPINE

ASSOCIATED WITH: LEGS, FEET, BONES, LARGE INTESTINE, AND ADRENAL GLANDS

THE BASE CHAKRA IS CLOSEST TO THE EARTH AND FUNCTIONS AS A CONNECTION TO PHYSICAL SURVIVAL. IT CONTROLS THE FIGHT-OR-FLIGHT RESPONSE. IF BLOCKAGES OCCUR, THEY MAY MANIFEST AS PARANOIA, FEAR, PROCRASTINATION, OR DEFENSIVENESS. THIS CHAKRA IS THE ENERGY CENTER THAT GROUNDS US. ALTHOUGH MOST PEOPLE HAVE HEARD OF THE SEVEN MAIN CHAKRAS, THERE ARE ACTUALLY 114 CHAKRAS IN THE HUMAN BODY, FORMING A COMPLEX ENERGY SYSTEM. IN ADDITION TO THE 114 CHAKRAS, THERE ARE 72,000 NADIS OR

ENERGY CHANNELS THROUGH WHICH ENERGY OR PRANA MOVES. EACH CHAKRA IS ASSOCIATED WITH CERTAIN PARTS OF THE BODY AND ORGANS, PROVIDING THE ENERGY NEEDED TO FUNCTION. THE BODY IS THE HOUSE THAT NOT ONLY HOLDS YOUR SPIRIT AND SOUL BUT ALSO STORES ENERGY THAT WORKS TO KEEP THE BODY ALIVE AND FUNCTIONING.

THE BODY, SPIRIT, AND SOUL USE THESE CHAKRAS TO PRODUCE ENERGY THAT CONNECTS TO ALL THE ORGANS, ALLOWING THE BODY TO MOVE. IT'S AMAZING HOW GOD CREATED THE HUMAN BODY, HOW THE BODY FUNCTIONS, AND HOW THE ENERGY THAT FLOWS THROUGH THE BODY WORKS IN HARMONY WITH THE SPIRIT, SOUL, CHAKRAS, AND ENERGY CENTERS WITHIN OUR ORGANS. THIS COMBINATION OF SPIRIT, SOUL, AND BODY IS WHAT MAKES US THE SUPERNATURAL HUMAN BEINGS THAT GOD CREATED FROM THE DUST OF THE GROUND.

THE HEART IS THE HOUSE OF THE SOUL.

CHAPTER 8:

BATTLING WITH THE SOUL

THIS IS THE WAY I BEGAN TO WAR WITHIN MY SOUL, MY FEELINGS AND EMOTIONS WERE CAUSING ME TO ACT OUT SO I BEGAN TO PRAY AND ASKED GOD TO HELP ME, LORD PLEASE HEAL MY HEART AND THE WOUNDS AND SCARS OF MY SOUL THIS WAS EASY, BECAUSE I STARTED HAVING ALL KINDS OF THOUGTS RUNNING THROUGH MY MIND, AND HAVING ALL THESE EMOTIONS FLOODING OUT OF ME, MY BEHAVIOR BEGIN TOO CHANGE. I JUST COULDN'T DEAL WITH MY FEELINGS, TRYING TO LOVE SOMEONE WHEN YOUR SOUL HAS A HOLE IN IT IS NEVER EASY. I WANTED TO RUN AWAY FROM WHAT I WAS FEELING. I DIDN'T WANT ANYONE TO KNOW THAT I WAS HURTING. I DIDN'T REALIZE THAT GOD HAD PLACED SOMEONE IN MY LIFE TO HELP ME HEAL FROM THE ABUSE OF MY PAST RELATIONSHIPS THAT I HAD BEEN HURT FROM. I WAS SCARED AND FEAR SET IN I THOUGHT I COULD CONTROL THIS KIND OF PAIN, BUT COULD NOT, I PRAYED THAT GOD WOULD TAKE THESE FEELINGS AWAY FROM ME, BUT I WAS BATTLING WITHIN MY HEART, BECAUSE I FOUND THE LOVE THAT I'VE

BEEN PRAYING FOR BUT BECAUSE MY HERAT WAS BROKEN AND MY SOUL HAD A HOLE IN IT. MY FEELINGS BEGAN TO CHANGE AND BECOME STRONGER.

IT FELT SO GOOD TO FEEL AND UNDERSTAND WHAT REAL LOVE A PERSON COULD SHARE WITH SOMEONE IF YOU DID NOT FORCE IT BUT ALLOWED THINGS TO HAPPEN NATURALLY. I ALLOWED MYSELF TO TRUST SOMEONE I CAME OUT OF MY SHELL AND LET SOMEONE IN TOO MY HEART. WHEN IT HIT ME I BEGAN TO PRAY TO GOD SAYING THAT YOU LOVE US UNCONDITIONALLY.

THAT WAS WHEN I BEGAN TO FEEL THE UNCONDITIONAL LOVE THAT GOD HAS FOR US ALL. BUT WE SOMETIMES REJECT GODS LOVE FOR US, WHEN WE DISOBEY HIM GOD WANTS US TO TOTALLY DEPEND ON HIM FOR EVERYTHING IN OUR LIVES.SO THAT WAS WHEN I REALIZED I WASN'T ALLOWING GOD TO TAKE CONTROL OVER THE THINGS I HAD NO CONTROL OF AND COULDN'T DO ANYTHING ABOUT. I REALIZED IF I WANTED TO BE HEALED, DELIVERED, AND SET FREE. I MUST TRUST GOD IN EVERY AREA OF MY LIFE. I BEGAN TO PRAY AND TALK TO GOD TELLING HIM I NEED YOU LORD GOD, IM DEPENDING ON YOU

LORD WHILE YOU RESTORE ME OF ALL SICKNESS IN MY BODY, MIND, AND SOUL. I PRAYED THAT GOD WOULD RESTORE ME PHYSICALLY, MENTALLY, EMOTIONALLY, SPIRITUALLY AND OR SEXUALLY.

GOD INSPIRED ME TO WRITE ABOUT THE HURT AND PAIN OF MY PAST. AS I BEGAN TO CRY AND WRITE THIS BOOK I BEGAN TO HEAL. I KNEW THAT I COULD LOVE AGAIN AND IT FELT GOOD, TO BE HEALED FROM THE THINGS OF MY PAST. I NOW WANTED TO LOVE AGAIN. I'M NOT GOING TO RUN AWAY FROM WHAT I WANTED AND NEEDED, AND THAT WAS LOVE. GOD PUT US HERE TO ENJOY OUR LIVES AND LOVE ONE ANOTHER. SO PLEASE ALLOW GOD TO HEAL YOU OF PAST HURT AND PAIN AND ALLOW HIM TO HEAL YOUR SOUL, ALLOW THE WOUNDS AND SCARS OF BAD RELATIONSHIPS TO BE HEALED, AND BE SET FREE TO LOVE AND LIVE A PEACEFUL LIFE IN JESUS NAME. MY SOUL NO LONGER HAS A HOLE IN IT. THE SOUL AND THE WOUNDS AND SCARES ARE HEALED. THANK YOU, LORD FOR HEALING MY SOUL OF

BIIERNESS, ANGER, UNFORGIVENESS, RESMORSE AND DOUBT. THANK YOU, LORD, FOR HEALING ME FROM NEGATIVE

EMOTIONS THAT THE DEVIL TRIED TO PLACE IN MY MIND TO CONTROL ME. I ALLOWED THE HOLY SPIRIT IN TO HEAL IN JESUS NAME. MY SOUL HAS BEEN HEALED, THANK YOU GOD. THANK YOU HOLY SPIRIT HAVE YOUR WAY IN MY LIFE AND LIFE OF

GOD PEOPLE IN JESUS NAME AMEN.

DEDICATION PAGE

I THANK GOD FOR ALLOWING OUR PATHS TO CROSS AND I THANK YOU FOR BEING IN MY LIFE ALWAYS ENCOURAGING ME AND SUPPORTING ME, THANK YOU FOR TEACHING ME ABOUT REAL LOVE, FOR YEARS I WOULD NOT ALLOW ANYONE TO GET CLOSE TO MY HEART, BECAUSE I HAD BEEN ABUSED SO BAD IN REALIONSHIPS THAT I NEVER WANTED TO DEAL WITH MY FEELINGS AND EMOTIONS, SO I BURIED THEM, THOSE FEELINGS AND THOUGHTS INTO MY UNCONSCIOUS MIND. I PUT UP A WALL AND IT BECAME THE SHELL I LIVED IN. I DID DEAL WITH PEOPLE WITHOUT ALLOWING THEM INSIDE MY HEART, SO THEY WOULD NEVER GET TO KNOW THE REAL ME. I PUT OUT A FALSE SENSE OF LOVE, BUT YOU SAID LOVE DIDN'T HURT ME IT WAS THE PEOPLE I WAS GIVING MY LOVE TO THAT HURT ME THE MOST, I ALLOWED YOU IN BUT STILL WAS TRYING TO KEEP THAT WALL UP WITH YOU AT FIRST.

THEN ONE DAY YOU TOLD ME TO ALLOW THINGS TO HAPPEN NATURALLY AND OUR FRIENDSHIP BEGAN. ALL THOSE BRICKS I USED TO BUILD UP THAT WALL AROUND ME, STARTED TO FALL AND I CAME OUT OF MY SHELL THAT HOUSED MY

FEELINGS FOR SO LONG. I NATURALLY FELL IN LOVE WITH YOU, BUT STILL DID NOT KNOW HOW TO REALLY LOVE ANYONE, BECAUSE MY FIRST REACTION TO HOW I WAS FEELING WAS I COULDN'T DO THIS ANYMORE, BECAUSE OF THE FEAR OF BEING HURT AGAIN. I BEGAN TO BATTLE WITH ALL OF THESE SUPPRESSED EMOTIONS THAT WERE ONCE LOCKED UP INSIDE OF MY UNCONSCIOUS MIND AND SOUL, NOT TELLING YOU WHAT I REALLY WAS FEELING. I WANTED TO TALK TO YOU ABOUT THESE FEELINGS, BUT I WAS AFRAID THAT YOU WOULDN'T WANT TO DEAL WITH SOMEONE WHOSE SOUL WAS WOUNDED AND ABUSED UNTIL I BEGAN TO FACE THESE FEELINGS I WOULD NEVER BE ABLE TO LOVE YOU OR NOBODY ELSE. I PRAYED BECAUSE ONCE AGAIN I WANTED TO RUN AWAY, BUT GOD BEGAN TO SHOW ME THAT I NEEDED TO DEAL WITH THE PAIN AND HURT OF MY PAST AND BECAUSE OF YOU I BEGAN TO WRITE THIS BOOK. MY SOUL HAS BEEN ABUSED, BEING ABLE TO EXPRESS TO YOU SOME OF THE THINGS I WAS FEELING, NOT WANTING YOU TO KNOW THAT I WAS A BROKEN WOMAN IN FEAR OF LOSING THE ONE PERSON WHO WAS HELPING ME HEAL, I EVEN TRIED TO WALK AWAY FROM YOU, I TRIED TO SABOTAGE OUR FRIENDSHIP, BECAUSE

I DIDNT WANT TO HAVE THESE FEELINGS, NOBODY IS SUPPOSE TO BE HERE AND ME FEELING THE WAY I DO ABOUT YOU.

I THOUGHT I COULD CONTROL WHAT I WAS FEELING. I BEGAN WARRING WITH MY FEELINGS FOR YOU, BUT YOU TOLD ME LOVE COMES AUTOMATICALLY AND I COULD CONTROL HOW I FELT AND ONCE AGAIN YOU WERE RIGHT. I CANT CONTROL THESE FEELINGS BECAUSE YOU CANT HELP THOSE YOUR HEART LOVES, BUT IT DID NOT STOP ME FROM HAVING THE FEAR OF LOSING YOU OR THAT YOU MAY NOT ALWAYS BE THERE FOR ME WHEN I NEEDED YOU AND THAT SCARED ME, BECAUSE NOT ONLY DID I NEED YOU I WANTED YOU IN MY LIFE. I NEVER WANTED TO EVER DEPEND ON ANYONE BUT I REALIZED I NEEDED YOU BECAUSE YOU WERE MAKING ME DEAL WITH MY FEELINGS. THE PAIN, HURT THAT HAD BECOME DEEP SCARES AND WOUNDS IN MY SOUL, THAT I HAD NEVER DEALT WITH UNTIL NOW. I THANK YOU FROM THE BOTTOM OF MY HEART FOR GIVING ME WHAT I NEEDED, LORD YOU SENT AN ANGEL OF LOVE, YOU ARE MY LOVE AGENT FROM GOD. I APPRECIATE YOU SO MUCH NO ONE HAS BEEN ABLE TO GET THIS CLOSE TO ME IN YEARS OR UNTIL NOW. I NEVER WANTED TO SHARE MY MOST INTIMATE DETAILS AND THOUGHTS. I

ONLY WANTED TO SHARE WHAT WAS ON THE SURFACE, NOT WHAT WAS DEEP DOWN INSIDE OF ME. YOU HAVE CHANGED MY LIFE, AND YOU'VE HELPED ME GET THROUGH THE WRITING OF MY FIRST BOOK, I DEDICATED THIS BOOK TO YOU, BECAUSE IF YOU HAD ENCOURAGED ME, I DO THINK I WOULD HAVE FINISHED THE FIRST BOOK I WROTE.

WINDOWS OF DELIVERANCE ON SPIRITUAL ABUSE. THANK YOU, MY LOVE AGENT, YOU WILL FOREVER HAVE MY HEART AND I WILL LOVE YOU FOREVER. I WILL KEEP BEING STRONG JUST LIKE YOU SAID. LOVE YA, MY LOVE AGENT. TO MY READERS I APPRECIATE YOU, I HOPE THIS BOOK MAY HAVE TOUCHED YOU IN A WAY THAT THIS LETTER IDENTIFIES WITH YOU IN SOME WAY. I HAVE PROVIDED AN EXATRA LINE FOR YOU TO NAME YOUR LOVE AGENT IF YOU SO CHOOSE

_______________________________.

POEM: A KING LEADS AND A QUEEN FOLLOWS.

A KING LEADS AND A QUEEN FOLLOWS A GOOD MAN IS WHAT SHE SEES WHEN SHE LOOKS AT YOU, IT IS SO MUCH MORE TO YOU THAT SHE SEES THAT A LOT OF PEOPLE CAN SEE. A QUEEN WILL FOLLOW YOU BECAUSE SHE SEES WHO YOU ARE AS A MAN, A REAL MAN A KING, THAT NEEDS A QUEEN TO BE BY HIS SIDE, WHO GOING TOO LOVE YOU AND NOT JUDGE YOU, WHO GOING TO UNDERSTAND THAT THE CHOICES THAT YOU MAKE IS ONLY TO MAKE LIFE SO MUCH EASIER FOR YOU BOTH. A QUEEN THAT STOP TALKING AND REALLY LISTEN TO WHAT YOU HAVE TO SAY. A QUEEN THAT GOING TO HELP YOU AS YOU FOLLOW YOUR DREAMS.

A QUEEN THAT IS ALWAYS PRAYING FOR YOU, SO SOMETIMES A KING MUST JUST STOP AND REFLECT ON WHO'S REALLY THERE. A QUEEN WANTS TO STAND BY A KING'S SIDE AND HELP HIM REACH HIS GOALS AND BE A PART OF ALL YOUR LIFE ACHIEVEMENT.

A QUEEN WHO'S GOING TO BE THERE THROUGH ALL YOUR UPS AND DOWNS. A KING WHO NEVER LOSES SIGHT AND REMEMBERS THAT THERE IS SOMEONE THAT BELIEVES IN YOU

TO LEAD HER AS SHE FOLLOWS, FOR SHE HAS FOUND HER KING, THE MAN THAT SHE PRAYED TO GOD FOR, A QUEEN WHOSE READY TO SUMMIT AND WAIT TO BE BY YOUR SIDE. A KING LEADS AND A QUEEN THAT IS READY TOO FOLLOW.

THIS BOOK ON MY SOUL HAS BEEN ABUSED, I WROTE IT BECAUSE I WAS HAVING PROBLEMS DEALING WITH MY FEELINGS, EMOTIONS AND THE PAIN OF CARRYING ALL THESE THOUGHTS AND FEELINGS INSIDE OF MY MIND, MY SOUL SO WOUNDED, WITH SCARES SO DEEP THAT I DIDNT KNOW HOW TOO TRUST AND LOVE WITHOUT BEING IN FEAR OF NOT ALLOWING PEOPLE IN MY LIFE WHO WANTED TO LOVE ME AND GET CLOSE TOO ME. I DID NOT KNOW WHAT REAL LOVE WAS UNTIL GOD PLACED SOMEONE IN MY LIFE THAT WOULD CHANGE HOW I FELT. I THANK YOU

GOD EVERY DAY FOR OPENING UP MY EYES SENDING ME AN ANGEL IN MY LIFE, AND EXPERIENCING REAL LOVE, GOD IS LOVE... AMEN

REFERENCES PAGE.

WIKIPEDIA.ORG

THE HOLY BIBLE KJB, NIB

HEALTHLINE. COM

WINDOWS OF DELIVERANCE ON SPIRITUAL ABUSE, JANRT K HOWARD

A SPIN-OFF OF BOOK ONI WINDOWS OF DELIEVENCES.

9 781966 190110